AVENGERS INFINITY WAR: THE HERO'S JOURNEY:
GUARDIANS OF THE GALAXY
A CENTUM BOOK 9781910114643

Published in Great Britain by Centum Books Ltd

This edition published 2018

1 3 5 7 9 10 8 6 4 2

Centum Books Ltd, 20 Devon Square, Newton Abbot, Devon, TQ12 2HR, UK

books@centumbooksltd.co.uk

CENTUM BOOKS Limited Reg. No. 07641486

A CIP catalogue record for this book is available from the British Library

Printed in the United Kingdom

ROAD TO AVENGERS: INFINITY WAR

MARVEL

AVENGERS
INFINITY WAR

THE HERO'S JOURNEY
GUARDIANS OF THE GALAXY

STEVE BEHLING

centum

PROLOGUE

Eclector M-ship GK9
N42U K11554800·520347
Day 1

There was a time when I didn't hate her. At least, I don't think I hated her. I remember... liking her. Looking up to her. Needing her.

She was the only person who knew exactly what I was going through. Who could feel what I was feeling. Who could relate to me.

Or so I thought.

It never occurred to me that someone could experience the same things you did, yet come away feeling completely different.

Of course I didn't know any of this back then. I'm just barely beginning to understand it all now.

As I advance toward my ultimate quest, my one true purpose, the sole reason for living—as I see it—I'm setting this down so I never forget what it's like to live a life in anger, consumed by hate, and lose nearly everything along the way—including myself.

My name is Nebula.

And I hate my sister.

CHAPTER ONE

Anger.

It lived within her, filling her with purpose. It colored everything in her life an uncompromising red.

So. Much. Anger.

Ask anyone who had ever crossed her path, and they would tell you the same thing: To say she was full of anger was like saying that the universe was full of stars.

It was and she was and that's all there was to it.

Period. End of story.

Except it wasn't the end of the story. Not hers. It was only the beginning.

• • •

Where it really all started was with a ship.

A hot mess of a ship, to be exact.

Nebula had noted her surroundings with disgust. Everything in the craft looked used...worn...dirty. Not "filthy" dirty, just...dirty. Like no one had bothered to clean the inside of the ship in who knew how long. Which, of course, they hadn't. It only made sense. Most people weren't going to take the time to clean the inside of a spaceship, especially when they were constantly being pursued across the galaxy.

She despised every second that she had spent handcuffed aboard The Milano. What a...meaningless name for a ship, she thought. It wasn't descriptive of its prowess. It certainly didn't inspire fear. And it definitely didn't sound like the name of a vessel that could rain destruction down upon any who would dare defy the will of its pilot and master.

So what kind of being would name their ship The Milano?

Peter Quill, that's who.

The self-proclaimed "Star-Lord."

She shook her head. How she ended up here, in

the custody of this...buffoon was beyond her. Handcuffed, no less. Confined to this ridiculous excuse for a ship while her sister and the rest of the so-called "Guardians of the Galaxy" prepared to bring Nebula to the planet Xandar.

Where she would spend the rest of her life locked away in a prison cell.

"You look..."

She turned, and looked at the person who had been standing next to her practically the whole time since she was brought on board. She didn't answer. Instead, she allowed her eyes—black, soulless—to communicate her thoughts. And they said, "I don't feel like talking right now. Or ever."

"...I was going to say tired."

She grunted in response to the tall, green-skinned woman standing before her. Gamora. Her sister. The look on her face seemed to suggest a...a kind of emotion. Something like...like...

...she confessed that she had no idea what it was. For years, she had allowed herself to feel only one emotion. She felt it so perfectly, so purely, that the emotion had practically consumed her, body and mind. It burned within her, an inferno charring her every thought, every action.

Maybe it was...tenderness? Caring? Concern? Whatever it was, she decided that she hated it. She had no use for any of those things. Not anymore.

To her, it was all a sign of weakness. And there was nothing that Nebula hated more than weakness.

"This ship," she said, changing the subject, "is a disaster. It's an unfortunate miracle you're still alive."

Gamora responded with a slight laugh, then walked a little closer. "It's a little better than that. It may not look like much, but it's home."

"Home," Nebula echoed. Somehow, in her mouth, the word became a curse. "How good that must feel, having a home."

"This again," Gamora said, sighing deeply. She let her head slump just a little, avoiding eye contact.

"Yes, 'this again!'" shouted Nebula. Her head

reared back in a sudden onslaught of rage, her black eyes wide, her mouth a contemptuous sneer, hands pulling against their restraints.

"I'm sorry," Gamora said after a long pause, picking up her head. The two locked eyes at last.

"I don't want your pity," Nebula spat out. Her voice was now cool and calm, striking a much different tone than the outburst of a few seconds ago. She was in control. Always in control.

Almost.

"Then what do you want?" Gamora asked.

"I want you dead."

"Sisters," Gamora said, then turned, and walked away.

• • •

"I am hungry," Nebula said, a hint of desperation in her voice. Hours had passed; she'd stopped keeping count of how many. "Hand me some of that yarrow root."

The handcuffs clicked into place on her wrists, now connected through a pole that extended from the ceiling. She was now confined to the crew's quarters, forced to stand for the duration of the trip.

"No," said the voice. "It's not ripe yet. And I hate you."

Nebula felt the blood boiling in her veins, her temples throbbing. "You hate me?" she said, not bothering to disguise her contempt or disgust. "You left me there while you stole that Stone for yourself. And yet here you stand. A hero."

The word "hero" stuck in her throat. It made her sick. She didn't need to specify where 'there' was. Gamora knew. It was the place the two sisters had been stuck in their entire lives, until Gamora had left and found a new family without so much as a backwards glance.

"I will be free of these shackles soon enough," Nebula continued. "And I will kill you. I swear."

"No," came the voice. "You're going to live out the rest of your days in a prison on Xandar. Wishing you could."

Nebula grunted, and yanked hard on the cuffs. They didn't budge, and neither did she.

CHAPTER TWO

Whether you're on Terra or Planet X, Xandar or Knowhere, there is one cosmic certainty that exists throughout the universe. Not death, although that's absolutely one (for the most part). And it's not taxes, although that's another (no exceptions).

No, the great cosmic certainty is this: Siblings argue. Maybe not all the time, but they argue. And sometimes, those arguments can get a little heated. People will say things, do things, in the heat of the moment. Even people who care deeply about one another—especially people who care deeply about one another—can turn from friend to foe in an instant. But when time passes and cooler heads prevail, they make their apologies, and reemerge, their familial bond even stronger.

At least, that's how most siblings handle things.

The same could not be said of Nebula and Gamora. When they had an argument, or even so much as felt one coming on, they would settle it the only way both women knew how, in a way only they could understand: each tried to break the fingers of the other.

Nebula remembered one such "argument," from a time when she and Gamora had both served their father's emissary, the Kree warrior known as Ronan the Accuser. Nebula had lived her entire life for their father, as had Gamora. Each wanted nothing more than to please him, to curry his favor. Unfortunately, their father was Thanos, a cosmic tyrant and dealer of death. One could not curry favor with a being who was never pleased and always disappointed.

Nothing Nebula did would ever please Thanos. He had impressed this upon her time and time again. She would never be good enough, never as good as Gamora.

From the moment Thanos put her and Gamora in Ronan's charge, Thanos made it clear: He expected great things from Gamora. He expected Nebula to perform her tasks, or die. No more, no less.

This hadn't sat well with Nebula.

So one day, she walked up behind her sister, seized her left arm, and twisted. Hard, until she grasped her hand, holding her fingers in her grip.

"You think I don't know?" she hissed. The anger boiled within her. It always boiled.

"Sister," Gamora said, her voice wrapped in pain. She winced as Nebula tightened her grip.

"You would keep me from advancing?" She squeezed Gamora's hand tighter, twisting, until there was a cracking sound. "You would have Ronan tell Father that only Gamora furthers his great plan...!"

Tighter and tighter Nebula squeezed, when suddenly, Gamora struck. Her right hand met Nebula's wrist, breaking her grip and causing Nebula to stagger. Gamora lashed out with her hand once more, this time striking Nebula firmly in the chest, knocking her back several feet.

"I will keep you alive!" Gamora said, an all-out battle between the women only a moment away.

They moved on one another, their faces only inches apart. Both expected the other to attack. Neither had.

Yet.

"Compassion?" Nebula said, her voice dripping with disdain. "What would Ronan say to that?" She had no compassion for her sister, or anyone else, for that matter. But she recognized it when she saw it.

Nebula thought she had shut down Gamora's pathetic attempt to...to do whatever it was she was attempting to do.

But she should have known better. As hard as Nebula pushed her sister away, Gamora dug in her heels even harder.

"Please, Nebula," Gamora whispered, desperately trying to reach her sibling. "You have known me since Thanos took us both from our homes as children. You have stood beside me...in training, in modification...in battle!"

Gamora was trying to appeal to her, Nebula thought. Too little, too late. She would let Gamora know the score between them.

"I have stood behind you," Nebula said, not giving any ground, "when I am every inch the warrior you are." She looked at her sister's face, and saw that what she was saying irritated her. She persisted. "The screams of my victims fill every field."

"That's because you take too long to kill them," Gamora answered.

The anger that burned within Nebula became an inferno.

With a savage growl, Nebula thrust her right hand toward Gamora, what should have been a killing blow. But her sister evaded the attack, instead grabbing Nebula by the throat with her right arm. Gamora shoved her up against a wall, hand tightening around her windpipe.

Nebula wondered if this was the day that at last Gamora would end her life.

But she knew better.

Gamora hesitated for a second.

One second was all the expert assassin needed to break her sister's hold, knocking the arm away.

Gamora seemed about to say something. For a moment, the two women stared into one another's eyes. Neither knew what was about to happen.

Then Gamora backed away, walking off into the darkness.

As quickly as the argument had begun, it was over.

And that's how it was between Nebula and Gamora.

CHAPTER THREE

Eclector M-ship GK9
N42U K115548U0·520356
Day 2

I look at my hand and I see fingers that cannot be broken. Well, the truth is they can. With great effort. But I will feel nothing. So it doesn't matter. Nothing matters.

Except killing my father.

I wonder what it's like to feel nothing? To be totally, completely numb. I don't know that I've ever experienced that. I don't know if I ever will.

Father saw to that.

He only had use for two feelings: Hate and fear. He instilled both in me. In us.

And now I hate and fear everything.

CHAPTER FOUR

With no fingers to break this time, and no one to talk to, Nebula was left inside the disheveled crew's quarters of The Milano, a prisoner—of her sister's, and of her own thoughts. She had nowhere to go, and plenty of time to reflect on how she had gotten there.

As often was the case, Nebula blamed her current circumstances on her sister. Had it not been for her, she reasoned, none of this would have happened in the first place. If Gamora had not prevented her from...

Nebula took a deep breath, and swallowed. She felt a lump in her throat. She wanted to hit something. No, not something. Someone. A particular green-skinned someone.

Her thoughts drifted to The Dark Aster, the ship upon which she and Gamora had served Ronan. Ronan was a fanatic. A Kree warrior who followed the ancient customs of his people with zealous devotion. One of those ancient customs included the preservation of a practically unending war against the people of Xandar, and its police force, the Nova Corps.

After more than a thousand years of fighting, the Kree and the Xandarians had at last signed a peace treaty between their people. It was an uneasy truce, but it held, much to Ronan's disgust. He ignored the treaty. His hatred of Xandar and its inhabitants drove him to more extreme measures. He wished Xandar to be cleansed, to be made pure...by ridding the universe of Xandarians entirely.

It wasn't enough that he had been attacking Xandarian colonies and outposts, slaughtering innocent people. He wanted to wipe the Xandarian plague out at the source.

To destroy Xandar itself.

To achieve this goal, he made a bargain with Nebula's father, Thanos. There was an object that Thanos desired—an orb. The Orb, a priceless artifact that housed the Power Stone. And when Thanos desired something, Nebula knew, he would not be denied. In exchange for retrieving the Orb and delivering it to Thanos, the warlord agreed to...

Nebula remembered exactly how it had transpired.

"Ronan," Nebula said flatly. "Korath has returned."

Korath was a Kree mercenary, working for Ronan. He had been charged with retrieving the Orb from a planet called Morag. And now, it appeared, he had returned with little other than words to show for it.

"Master," Korath said hastily, as he entered Ronan's chamber aboard The Dark Aster. "He is a thief! An outlaw who calls himself 'Star-Lord.'"

That was the first time Nebula had heard the name "Star-Lord." It sounded ridiculous to her then, too.

Ronan was impassive, unmoved. Korath continued, half explaining, half seeking forgiveness. "We have discovered he has an agreement to retrieve the Orb for an intermediary known as the Broker."

The Broker operated from a location on Xandar

itself. Korath clearly hoped delivering this slim lead might mitigate Ronan's anger.

Nebula stood by, watching, waiting to see how the Accuser would react.

Spoiler alert: he didn't take it well.

"I promised Thanos I would retrieve the Orb for him," Ronan said, his breathing even. "Only then will he destroy Xandar for me."

Nebula wondered if and when Ronan would crush Korath's skull.

"Nebula!" Ronan shouted, impulsively. She turned her head, and looked directly at him. "Go to Xandar and get me the Orb."

So. Korath had fallen out of Ronan's favor, Nebula thought. Now it is my turn. Not Gamora's. Mine.

"It will be my honor," Nebula said. But before she could exit Ronan's presence and begin her journey, someone else spoke.

"It will be your doom."

Gamora.

Nebula could hardly hear anything else for the sound of her pulse thundering in her ears.

"This happens again, you'll be facing our father without his prize," Gamora said, calmly.

Nebula could feel her anger rising. Gamora suggested that Nebula would fail. She always did that. Always had to win.

Every time an opportunity came along to prove to Thanos who was more worthy, who was more capable, who was the better warrio —every time, Gamora had to try and show her up. It was a never-ending competition between the two. A competition with very real, dire consequences. For Nebula, at least.

"I'm a daughter of Thanos," Nebula said, the words uttered from behind clenched teeth. "Just like you."

"But I know Xandar," Gamora replied.

Nebula could practically feel Ronan changing his mind. "Ronan has already decreed that I—"

"Do not speak for me!" Ronan thundered. He

turned his gaze from Nebula, and focused squarely on Gamora. "You will not fail."

"Have I ever?" Gamora said.

And so it happened. In a matter of seconds, Gamora had stolen another opportunity from her, another chance to prove to their father what she could do.

Nebula suddenly felt a strong desire to break some fingers.

CHAPTER FIVE

There was nothing for Nebula to do while Gamora traveled to Xandar in pursuit of the Orb. Nothing to do but wait. For a warrior like Nebula, waiting was a dull, tedious business. Excruciating. And waiting on The Dark Aster was as unpleasant as it was dull.

Nebula saw the Sakaaran mercenaries that Ronan employed as mindless insects, living only to serve the hive. They didn't speak unless spoken to, and they obeyed every order they were given, regardless of whether they might live or die.

It would only be later that Nebula would realize that the reason she loathed the Sakaaran because they reminded her of herself.

A part of Nebula—a very large part of her—had hoped that Gamora would fail on her mission to retrieve the Orb. That something catastrophic would happen to her sister on Xandar's surface, and she would either return empty handed, like Korath, or—even better—not return at all. Then she would be able to turn to Ronan and say, "Look! She has failed you! I would never have let that happen. Only I can obtain the Orb for Thanos!"

But that was fantasy, and Nebula knew it.

If Gamora failed to seize the Orb, then her failure would become Ronan's failure...would become Nebula's. For they would have to report to Thanos that they had been unable to secure the Orb. Thanos' anger would be great. And in a fit of anger, Thanos would mete out his punishments.

Nebula had been on the receiving end of those punishments for years.

They'd made her who she was, for better or—more likely—for worse.

"She will return with the Orb," Ronan reasoned. The Accuser contemplated the massive war hammer he held in his hands. "To do otherwise means death."

"That's for Thanos to decide," Nebula said. "Not Ronan."

Ronan shot Nebula a look that would have frozen any other being in fear, stopped them where they stood.

Nebula was not "any other being."

While she was there to serve Ronan's whims, just like Gamora, she knew that ultimately, nothing would happen to her unless Thanos allowed it. For Ronan to attack her or her sister without Thanos' approval would bring swift, violent retribution from Thanos himself. Ronan knew it, too.

Ronan grunted. "Gamora's success belongs to Thanos. Her failure does not. You know as well as I the price of failure."

Nebula thought about that for a moment. "I know it better," she said, tapping her left arm with a finger. The metallic ping resonated in her ears.

CHAPTER SIX

Eclector M-ship GK9
N42U K11554800·520405
Day 6

I do remember some things. Mostly bad.

I remember what it was like to hear. To actually hear sound. Instead of having circuitry interpret sound into something meaningful.

Another gift from my father.

Did you know he replaced my ears, because I failed to respond to him once?

Once.

I was a child. Alone, for the first time. Thanos demanded I speak my name.

I was...terrified of him. I felt powerless. I could not speak.

He did not repeat himself. He ordered one of his Sakaaran worms to box my ears.

That was the last real sound I remember.

CHAPTER SEVEN

Gamora had not reported back since she'd arrived on Xandar. Hours passed, and it soon became clear—to Nebula, at least—that she wasn't going to come back. Not with the Orb, at any rate.

Where Nebula saw things in three dimensions, Ronan saw only two. So he was blindsided when The Dark Aster intercepted the reports coming in via interspace wire that Gamora had been apprehended by the Nova Corps on Xandar. She had been taken into custody along with several others.

Nebula trained The Dark Aster's communications relay toward Xandar, and tapped into the transmission. She watched the feed with great interest. While she couldn't see the Nova officers in the feed, she could see the image of her sister clear enough. Captured, like a common criminal. A thug in a police lineup.

Pathetic.

"Gamora," came the officer's voice over the transmission. "Surgically modified and trained as a living weapon. The adopted daughter of the mad Titan Thanos."

'Surgically modified,' Nebula thought. How easy it was to reduce Thanos' cruelty to two simple words.

"Recently, Thanos lent her and her sister Nebula out to Ronan, which leads us to believe that Thanos and Ronan are working together."

"Leads us to believe...?" Nebula realized that Gamora had not told the Nova Corps anything. If she had, they would have known for absolute certain that Thanos was employing Ronan to achieve his ends.

That meant they also didn't know about the Orb.

The Nova officer continued. "Subject 89P13. Calls itself Rocket. The result of illegal genetic and cybernetic experiments on a lower life form."

Subject 89P13 looked like...Nebula wasn't sure

what it looked like. An animal of some kind. Like none she had ever encountered before. It stood upright on its hind legs, and wore clothes. A strange, furry beast.

"What the hell?" said one of the Nova officers as the next detainee stepped into view.

"They call it Groot," said another officer. "A humanoid plant that's been traveling recently as 89P13's personal houseplant-slash-muscle."

This "Groot" looks like a walking tree, Nebula thought. She had heard of his species before, but hadn't seen one until this moment.

She watched as Groot walked away, and a human took his place. He had short brown hair, a scruffy looking beard, and wore a leather jacket.

"Peter Jason Quill. From Terra," said the officer. "Raised from youth by a band of mercenaries called the Ravagers, led by Yondu Udonta."

Nebula watched, repulsed and yet somewhat fascinated by what the Terran was doing with his hands. He held his left hand closed, turned up, in a fist. With his right hand, he simulated a cranking motion? What was he doing?

She had never met a Terran before, and decided based on this alone that they were all useless and beneath her.

The transmission cut out, and Nebula was left wondering: Where were the Nova Corps taking Gamora now? And was the Orb in her possession?

CHAPTER EIGHT

It had been a simple matter to find out where the Nova Corps were taking Gamora and her conspirators. By hacking into the Nova communications system, Nebula learned that they were being transported to the Kyln, a high-security Xandarian prison.

While she was obtaining this information, Nebula saw an incoming transmission from the Sanctuary.

The domain of Thanos.

"Dad's calling," Nebula said. "This should be interesting."

• • •

Inside Ronan's spartan chamber aboard The

Dark Aster, the transmitted image of Thanos' emissary raged.

"You have been betrayed, Ronan!" the robed figure boomed. The thing's face sneered at the Kree warrior.

"We know only that she has been captured," Ronan said, trying to assert himself. "Gamora may yet recover the Orb."

Off to the side, Nebula stood and watched. *Ronan wishes to show my father that he's in charge,* she thought, amused. *He needn't bother.*

"No!" shouted the emissary. "Our sources within the Kyln say Gamora has her own plans for the Orb."

Then she does have it, Nebula thought. *Hidden somewhere, on the Kyln?*

"Your partnership with Thanos is at risk."

Ronan's eyes went wide, and he looked at the emissary with unbridled fury. Before he could speak, the emissary ended their conversation.

"Thanos requires your presence. Now!"

The transmission faded. In its place, a glowing

light appeared, which grew taller and wider in seconds. The light within soon faded to the edges of a circle. Within the circle, Nebula could see the stars and asteroids that marked Thanos' domain. Ronan glared at Nebula, summoning her to his side.

The two walked through the glowing circle, and entered the Sanctuary.

As their feet crossed the rocky terrain of an asteroid, behind them, the glowing portal faded away. In front of them was a small arena-like structure of rocks. Thanos' robed emissary stood off to one side. Behind him, there was an enormous throne, floating just above the ground. Though the throne was turned in the opposite direction, Nebula knew very well that Thanos sat upon it.

Waiting.

Ronan approached the emissary, as Nebula walked off to the side, and sat down upon a large boulder. Opening a panel on her left arm, Nebula looked inside at the circuitry and wires contained within.

More machine than woman.

She reached for a laser tool in her pocket, and started to make adjustments to the arm while she waited for Thanos' emissary to address them.

"With all due respect, Thanos, your daughter made this mess, and yet, you summon me,"

Immediately, Nebula looked up and shot a glance at Ronan. He had spoken first. She knew the protocol in dealing with her father. Speak when spoken to, and not a moment prior. What Ronan had just done, speaking before the emissary had addressed them, simply wasn't permitted. There were penalties for such behavior.

True enough, the emissary fumed. "I would lower my voice, Accuser!" he chided.

Before the emissary could say another word, Ronan said, "First, she lost a battle with some primitive."

"Thanos put Gamora under your charge!" the emissary shouted.

Ronan seemed not to notice, or not to care. "Then she was apprehended by the Nova Corps," he said, calmly.

Nebula looked down at her arm, and listened as

she fixed a power relay within her forearm. Dad's not going to like this, she thought.

"You are the one here with nothing to show for it!" the emissary growled.

The Accuser turned toward the emissary, unleashing his fury. "Your sources say that she meant to betray us the whole time!" Ronan screamed.

"Lower your tone!" the emissary warned.

Nebula listened, glancing up to see what would happen next. She saw Ronan unleash a burst of force from the Cosmi-Rod weapon he carried. It somewhat resembled a huge, heavy hammer. The Cosmi-Rod blast caught the emissary full in the face, killing him instantly. His corpse fell over, backward.

"I only ask that you take this matter seriously," Ronan said, satisfied that he had stated his case quite clearly.

Dad's really not going to like this, Nebula thought, shaking her head.

Slowly, the enormous throne began to turn

around, revealing Thanos' tremendous, bulky form. His skin was like stone, and there was fire in his eyes. He opened his ridged jaw slowly, as he leaned forward. At last he began to speak. "The only matter I do not take seriously, boy, is you."

Ronan was suddenly quiet. Nebula wasn't surprised.

"Your politics bore me," Thanos continued. He was so huge, he practically dwarfed the throne upon which he sat. He looked like he could crush it easily with either of his enormous hands. "Your demeanor is that of a pouty child. And apparently, you alienated my favorite daughter, Gamora."

There it was, Nebula thought with a roll of her black eyes. Just like her father to never miss a chance to let Nebula know that she was less than. Not as good as.

Thanos looked at Ronan, who remained motionless, speechless. A sort of twisted smile crept up on one side of his mouth. "I shall honor our agreement," Thanos said, "if you bring me the Orb."

Ronan waited expectantly.

Nebula knew exactly what was coming.

"But return to me again empty-handed," Thanos said, his voice remarkably even, "and I will bathe the starways in your blood."

Thanos leaned back in his throne. It was clear that their audience had ended. Nebula closed the compartment on her arm, and leapt off the boulder she was sitting on.

"Thanks, Dad," she said. "Sounds fair." This was nothing new to her. Standard operating procedure for her father.

Ronan stood, transfixed, not sure what to do next. Nebula walked toward him. Then, as she was closer, she said in a hushed voice, "This is one fight you won't win."

"Let's head to the Kyln," she said, trying to sound as nonchalant as possible.

CHAPTER NINE

Eclector M-ship GK9
N42U K11554800•520428
Day 11

I used to call him "Dad."

I said it to mock him.

I shouldn't have done that.

A dad is someone who takes care of you. It's someone who...

loves you.

He didn't take care of me. He never loved me.

I was a tool. Something to be used, when it served his purpose.

Maybe...I think I called him "Dad" as a kind of rebellion. Mocking him quietly, in soft words only I could hear. In my head. It was safe.

Thanos could not take that away from me.

But now I see that calling him "Dad" even in mockery was wrong. To do even that was to subscribe to Thanos' warped version of the truth.

CHAPTER TEN

But by the time The Dark Aster emerged from subspace and arrived at the orbiting Kyln, it was already too late. Nebula knew it. Gamora and her compatriots were long gone. They left behind them a prison in a state of complete and utter disarray.

Nebula was among the first to enter the Kyln. Once inside, she found herself floating within its dim, dingy halls, her path illuminated solely by emergency lighting.

"Status." Nebula heard the voice over her comms link. Ronan.

"No power. No gravity. They must have taken down the grid," Nebula replied.

"Restore both," Ronan ordered.

Nebula bit her lip.

She floated down the hall, pushing off the walls in a zig-zag fashion to propel her forward, until she came to a small workstation just outside the main prison level. Locating a control panel, she set about restoring the prison's artificial gravity, and at least basic power. It took a few minutes, but with a loud bang, the power—and along with it, the gravity field—kicked back in. From all around, she could hear the sound of objects that had once been floating now slam onto hard metal floors.

While she was at the controls, she accessed data files from the last hour to see what had transpired at the Kyln. Somehow, Gamora and her companions had seized control of the watchtower in the most heavily guarded area of the prison. Then, they must have disabled the prison's artificial gravity, and found a way to disconnect the watchtower from its stationary position. They managed to use the floating watchtower as a means of escape.

The prisoners had essentially turned the prison against their captors.

Nebula wouldn't allow herself to be impressed, but somewhere, there was a faint glimmer of pride that a member of her family had been involved in such an ingenious plan.

No. It wasn't pride. It was jealousy.

As she set foot inside the main holding area, Nebula saw beings in orange jumpsuits, sprawled everywhere. The prisoners. Many of them had shaved heads. Most of them looked like they had been battered, first by the guards trying to restore order, then by the station itself, when it lost gravity.

Then there were the Nova Corps officers, the guards. They, too, were there, trying to round up the prisoners, and corral them back into their cells.

The prisoners were no doubt disappointed that they had not been freed during Gamora's escape. Perhaps when they see me, Nebula thought, they'll think I'm here to free them. How wrong they are.

As Nebula watched, Ronan and several of his minions swept into the main holding area. At once, they commenced to interrogate the prisoners and the Nova Corps, trying to find a clue as to where Gamora was heading.

Nebula had borne witness to much brutality since her childhood, in the service of Thanos. What she saw that day at the Kyln exceeded it.

Ronan's minions broke bones, punctured lungs, snapped spines, and tortured the prisoners and the guards. No one knew anything. The threat—and execution—of bodily harm set no one talking, because no one had anything to say. At least not anything that was of value to Ronan.

Nebula thought they were telling the truth. There was nothing further to be gained by pressing their attack against the helpless people on the Kyln. But Ronan was relentless. The less people talked, the more he ordered Nebula and his minions to interrogate.

During the last such interrogation of a Nova

Corps officer, even Nebula's penchant for violence began to wear thin.

"I swear!" screamed the officer. "I don't know where they went! I swear!"

Nebula sighed. She had the officer's head trapped between two blades, and pushed them against his throat. "If he knew where they were, he would have already told us," Nebula said in frustration. They were getting nowhere.

"Ronan..." Nebula tried again to reason with him. Suddenly, she stopped and listened. She was receiving a communication from The Dark Aster. Bad news.

"The Nova Corps has sent a fleet to defend the prison," she said. The Dark Aster had detected the incoming fleet of Xandarian fighters. They had only minutes before the Kyln would be crawling with the Nova Corps.

"Well then," Ronan said, turning his attention away from Nebula. "Send Necro-Craft to every corner of the quadrant. Find the Orb. Any means. Any price."

He stormed off, heading back to The Dark Aster.

"And this place?" Nebula asked, looking around at the Kyln.

"Nova can't know what we're up to," he said. "Cleanse it."

Nebula had worked with Ronan long enough to know what "cleanse" meant. The prisoners and the guards had no idea.

But they would.

CHAPTER ELEVEN

Eclector M-ship GK9
N42U K11554800·520471
Day 15

I did not enjoy what I did on the Kyln. Those prisoners...they did not choose to be a part of my...obsession with my sister. They were caught in the middle.

I could have done something. Maybe? Convinced Ronan that they did not need to die. Spared them.

Saved them.

Why didn't I?

It's strange. I've never felt remorse over my actions before.

Perhaps having been imprisoned by the Sovereign has something to do with it. When I was their captive, I thought...what if they do to me, what I did to the prisoners on the Kyln?

Would they be as cold and unfeeling as me?

I have been a prisoner in so many ways.

CHAPTER TWELVE

Nebula stood up as straight as she could, stretched, and arched her back. Her hands remained cuffed to the pole inside the crew's quarters. She couldn't sit. She was tired, restless. Angry.

Hungry.

She heard a commotion coming from the flight deck above her. There was the booming voice of the man covered in tattoos, the one they called Drax, yelling something at Quill. The little rodent shouted something, too. They called it Rocket, she thought. It was difficult to make out the words over the sound of the ship's engines, but she could tell that the conversation was heated.

Something about the Sovereign. She knew a thing or two about them.

She laughed bitterly.

After the Orb incident, Nebula realized that in order for her to truly live, Thanos must die. In order to accomplish that, she would need weapons. In order to aquire weapons, she would need money That pursuit led her to the Sovereign homeworld. Their Anulax batteries were known throughout the galaxy as being one of the purest, most powerful sources of energy. If she could steal just a few, surely they would bring a handsome sum in the black market. Enough for her to purchase her own warship to destroy Thanos.

Of course, Nebula had not counted on getting caught.

Or becoming the Sovereign's prisoner.

Or pawn.

Something to be bartered with. Handed over to her sister, Gamora, in exchange for protecting their precious batteries from the Abilisk, power-hungry creatures intent on absorbing their energy.

Her wrist ached. The right one. Not her left wrist. That one never ached.

Ever since her real left arm had been replaced with its cybernetic equivalent, it could feel no pain. The arm didn't hurt. It never grew tired. And it could crush another being with just a thought.

Another gift from daddy dearest, she thought bitterly.

With the cold metal of what was now her left hand, she rubbed her right wrist. Her touch was surprisingly delicate. Nebula grimaced as she looked down at the handcuff squeezing into her flesh. When Gamora had placed the bonds on her, she clamped them down far too tight. Like she knew that it would hurt, and wanted Nebula to suffer.

Of course she knew it would hurt. So like her sister. Always having to prove a point.

Her stomach growled. How long had it been since she had eaten anything? Days?

Her hunger and the bowl of not-yet-ripe yarrow root reminded Nebula of an incident from her childhood. Something that had happened between her and Gamora. It seemed like forever ago. Nebula was a different person then.

Literally.

It was years ago. Back when she was still just a girl. So was Gamora. They had only recently been "adopted" by Thanos. Their real families had been killed, the girls taken away by Thanos to live their lives in servitude to him. Unsure of their place, or if they'd even survive, the girls had tried to support one another, to stick by each other. At first.

But Thanos would have none of that. He kept his children squabbling, scrapping against one another. That way, they would be so busy trying to win over the other that they would never be able to turn against him.

Early on, Thanos had decided that his "parenting" strategy would consist of two things: The threat of punishment for those who failed him, and the promise of reward for those who succeeded...or punished others. So he would pit one daughter against the other, in a series of never-ending competitions. Whether it was under the guise of training for battle, being taught the most deadly assassination techniques, or learning how to use exotic weapons, Thanos found a way to force the girls to fight against one another.

It was survival of the fittest. The girls were fearful of Thanos, and afraid of one another. Afraid of what might happen to them if they lost.

It may have been a brilliant way to train an individual to become a killing machine.

But it was a terrible, awful way to raise a child.

There was one such occasion, where the girls had been forced to battle repeatedly over three days. During this time, they were allowed only a small ration of water at regular intervals, and one half-hour of sleep each day. But no food.

As the fight wore on, and one day dragged into

the next, the girls became more and more tired, their bodies exhausted. They desperately needed food.

Then three days became four.

Then five.

At last, on the sixth day, Thanos promised that the girls would have some sustenance. Rather, one of them would. Whoever won that day's battle, he decreed, would have a piece of yarrow root.

Not a whole yarrow root. Just a piece.

But that was incentive enough to spark the young Nebula into white-hot fury. She had attacked her sister with such ferocity that day, that she had surprised even herself. Nebula fought like a demon possessed, never letting up.

Even at that young age, Gamora was already a skilled warrior, showing signs of the greatness she would one day achieve. This day, however, belonged to Nebula. She was relentless, until at last, Gamora fell before her.

Her sister at her feet, Nebula was torn. On the one hand, she had defeated her sister, and won the reward promised by her father. On the other, she felt sorry for Gamora. Both girls were starving. Nebula resolved that she would share the yarrow root with Gamora.

Then Thanos called to Nebula, ordering her to deliver the killing blow. She wasn't sure what to do. She felt compassion for her sister, but knew that to defy her father would incur his wrath. So she raised her weapon, and just as she was about to strike, Thanos grabbed her hand.

"Well done," he said, and for the first time since she had come under Thanos' care, Nebula felt like she had achieved something. Done something to make her father proud.

Until she realized that Thanos wasn't talking to her.

"Get up, Gamora," he said. "You must be hungry." Then he handed not a piece of yarrow root to her, but the whole yarrow root.

Nebula stood there in stunned silence.

"But father," she said in disbelief. "I won."

"Did you?" Thanos asked. "You were weak. Soft. You would have let Gamora live. Had the tables been turned, Gamora would not have hesitated to kill you. Let this be a lesson," Thanos said over his shoulder, as he walked away with Gamora, contentedly munching on the yarrow root. "The universe is unfair. Cold. Unforgiving. You would do well to remember that."

Gamora had apparently already taken a page from her father's playbook. She didn't look back at Nebula once, slumping to the cold ground in her weakened state. Didn't offer her a bite of the yarrow root she hadn't earned.

Nebula had laid on the ground convulsing with hunger, and cursed herself for her weakness. She had learned Thanos' lesson very well that day.

So well, in fact, that she had become just like the universe.

CHAPTER THIRTEEN

Gamora was to blame. For every awful, terrible thing that had ever happened to her. Of this, Nebula was certain.

She had kept her vow to be as cold and unforgiving as the universe. She allowed herself to neither show nor feel any emotion.

Save for one.

She had embraced anger, let it fill her every waking moment. Let it guide her every action and color her every decision. That would be her sustenance. It would nourish her throughout all the trials and tribulations of her childhood. As she matured, and the competitions between her and Gamora grew ever more bloodthirsty, Nebula harnessed that anger. It drove her to acts so savage and brutal that she scarcely recognized the person she had become.

She cared only about winning. No, not just winning. Surviving.

She would survive, above all else—or anyone else.

Aboard The Dark Aster, they had been searching the galaxy for signs of the Orb. After leaving the Kyln, Ronan had scattered his minions in pursuit of the artifact. So far, they had turned up with nothing. The galaxy was full of countless haystacks; it was nearly impossible that Ronan's armies should find the one that harbored the particular needle for which they were searching.

"Have you never wondered why Thanos desires the Orb?" Nebula asked Ronan.

The Kree warrior stared out into space. He didn't turn to look at Nebula. "It is not my place to wonder," Ronan answered. "I do as I must, so Thanos will deliver on his word."

Nebula tapped on her left forearm. "I see," she said. Others had served her father before. Few did for very long. Ronan had lived this long without questioning Thanos. Nebula wondered if that would prove to be his downfall.

• • •

Then a strange thing happened. The Dark Aster received a transmission from Knowhere. A galactic outpost that had been built inside the severed head of a colossal being known as a Celestial, Knowhere was home to some of the galaxy's less reputable elements. The outpost was a hotbed of illegal activity, gambling, and more.

And, if the transmission was any indication, it was currently providing shelter for a furious, tattooed individual named Drax.

"Ronan!" the man shouted over the transmission. He wasn't steady on his feet, and he swayed when he spoke. "Come to Knowhere and face your death!"

Nebula watched with interest as Ronan cocked his head curiously.

Drax staggered a bit, then opened his mouth, but didn't say anything. Then the transmission cut out.

Ronan turned to look at Nebula.

"That is the man the prisoners back on the Kyln described," she said. "The one who helped Gamora escape. If he is on Knowhere, then she is there, too."

"Then the Orb is there," Ronan replied. "Summon everyone. We go to Knowhere."

• • •

The fleet descended upon the dark and dingy world of Knowhere, and the denizens on the streets below scattered.

Save one.

Nebula watched as the ramp to Ronan's ship opened onto the street. She followed behind him, watching as the man they called Drax with the tattoos stood before them.

He wasn't swaying anymore.

"Ronan the Accuser!" Drax proclaimed. He brandished a large blade in each hand.

The Kree warrior walked forward, his head turned slightly, staring at Drax. His gaze was unwavering. "You are the one who transmitted the message?" he said.

"You killed my wife," Drax stated, his chest heaving. "You killed my daughter!"

Years ago, Nebula might have felt sorry for Drax, knowing that he was mere moments away from a terrible defeat at the hands of Ronan. Now, she felt nothing.

Because she had seen her sister.

There, in the distance, behind Drax, was Gamora. Her sister slid into a mining pod, a small, roundish vehicle, and soared into the sky accompanied by two other pods.

Nebula seethed.

"It is Gamora!" she said, interrupting Ronan. "She is escaping, with the Orb!"

"Nebula," Ronan said, as Drax began to attack. Ronan hardly seemed to notice, evading the tattooed man's strikes with ease. "Retrieve the Orb."

She ordered Ronan's minions to her side, and returned to Ronan's ship. Blasting off as Ronan continued the very one-sided battle against Drax, she took to the skies, in pursuit of the three mining pods.

Weaving through the sky, Nebula scanned the vehicles. The energy signal coming from the pod that was furthest away was almost frightening in its intensity, and she knew why. The signal was coming from the Orb. From inside the Orb.

An Infinity Stone. An object of immense power, it was one of six such Stones in existence. Thanos desired the Stones above all else. He was willing to lay waste to planets to find them.

"The Stone is in the furthest pod," she said, her eyes never leaving Gamora's one-person ship. "Bring it down!" she ordered.

The fighters flanking either side of the ship opened fire.

CHAPTER FOURTEEN

Eclector M-ship GK9
N42U K11554800•520471
Day 23

I wanted to succeed. To get the Stone. For Thanos.

And I wanted her dead.

I wanted both things so badly. That was my chance. Right there, on Knowhere. She was in my sights.

I fired on her with abandon. I ordered others to do the same.

Why?

Killing her wouldn't solve anything. I see that now.

It wouldn't make Father accept me. Bringing the Stone to him wouldn't make him love me.

I fired on her.

And then...long after...after the incident with the Sovereign...when I was my sister's captive...I knew what it was to be fired upon.

I didn't like it.

CHAPTER FIFTEEN

BOOM.

The Milano suddenly began to shake violently, jolting Nebula. Each roll of the craft sent Nebula this way and that, and each time, she was caught by the handcuff on her right wrist, digging in deeper. She grimaced, and felt a burning sensation as the pain added fuel to the simmering anger she felt inside.

She could only catch bits and pieces of the conversation from the flight deck, but by now it was clear that The Milano was under attack by enemy vessels. From her vantage point, or rather, lack of one, Nebula could see nothing. All she could do was feel the ship veer left or right, up or down, at breakneck speed.

Laser fire lashed the hull, and Nebula flinched as one blast tore into the ship's port side. There was an explosion. From inside the crew's quarters, it sounded like certain disaster had befallen The Milano.

From all the yelling and commotion on the flight deck, Nebula assumed that Quill was the one doing the flying. She decided that he was either a terrible pilot and was going to get them all killed, or he was a very skilled one, doing his best to avoid that fate. Right now, she wasn't sure which was the case.

As the battle raged, a thought struck Nebula. She realized there was a battle now taking place in which she could play no part. An event in which all her cunning, her ferocity, her warrior prowess, would not help her. All she could do was stand there, helpless, and get tossed around along with the ship.

She yearned for revenge against her sister. Her whole life had been spent in pursuit of proving herself better than Gamora. But now, the very real prospect existed that she might be killed along with everyone else aboard The Milano. There would be no revenge. The anger that had kept her alive for all these years would disappear along with her.

The thought filled her with a certain dread. She knew nothing in her life except toiling for Thanos, and striving to supplant her sister in her father's eyes. To have all that wiped out, to have any chance at settling the score against Gamora ripped from her, to forgo the opportunity for her father and sister to at last see her as equals, evoked another feeling in Nebula that she never could have expected.

Emptiness.

And then...

...sadness.

More laser fire rocked the ship, and threw Nebula downward. She felt the tug on her wrist, and her knees buckled. Losing her footing for just a second, Nebula found herself dangling from the handcuffs on the metal post. Quickly righting herself, she looked around, yanked on the handcuff again, unable to move.

Why should I be sad? Nebula thought. It had

been so long since she felt that way, if she could even remember, truthfully. Not since she was a little girl, torn from her family and her life, forced to live with Thanos. Forced to compete against the only person who she called "sister."

• • •

"You just have to tuck your head in when you roll, and it's really easy," Gamora said.

The young girl finished her demonstration by rolling, her head tucked in. When she came out of her roll, she sprung right to her feet, holding a long blade in her hands. She made a slashing motion to the right, then to the left.

Nebula watched, sullen. She kicked at a rock with her right foot.

"Easy for you," she said petulantly. "If I try and get it wrong—"

"You won't," Gamora interrupted, setting the blade down on the ground. "I'll help you."

They were in the Sanctuary, training on the rocky surface of an asteroid. It seemed like months since the day both girls had come to live there, since they had come to call Thanos Father. In reality, it was probably more like days. Time spent in the company of Thanos had a way of seeming like forever.

"Why would you help me?" Nebula asked. "Thanos—"

"Father," Gamora corrected.

"—Father wants us to try and beat each other. We should be opponents, not friends."

"Opponent, friend," Gamora said with a dismissive wave of her hand. "We are sisters first. I will look out for you."

Nebula responded with a small, shy smile. "Always?" she asked.

"Always. Now let me show you that roll."

CHAPTER SIXTEEN

Eclector M-ship GK9
  N42U K11554800•520471
  Day 23

I haven't thought about that moment in years. Maybe ever.

It may be the only happy memory I have from my childhood. The only moment that I could really CALL "childhood."

It was one of the only times that Gamora and I interacted that didn't involve some kind of competition. Or pain.

Thanos had watched every second.

He saw to it that there were no more such moments.

Gamora...my sister...the only other person alive who could possibly know what I have gone through. Who could even begin to understand.

Such distance between us. And yet...

Knowing what I know now...

...why did I pull the trigger so hard?

CHAPTER SEVENTEEN

The ship was still under fire, and showed no signs of slowing down.

Nebula cursed. She wanted to end this, right here, right now. Gamora raced ahead in the mining pod, outflying the Sakaaran fighters that accompanied Nebula. Even though the pod had no weapons, it was practically indestructible. It could take a hit. More than that, the pod could smash through practically anything and remain unharmed.

Like other ships, for instance.

Gamora's companions—Quill and the rodent— were flying two other mining pods, and wreaking havoc with Ronan's fighters. One of the pods kept barreling through the ships, one after the other, destroying them with blinding speed. Nebula winced as she saw the craft smash into buildings, explode, their occupants expiring.

Every time Gamora evaded her, every time the mining pod survived another shot, Nebula felt her heart beat faster. Her chance to stop Gamora and retrieve the Orb was dwindling, the window closing. If Gamora were to escape, it would mean a horrible punishment at the hands of Thanos.

At long last, Nebula began to close the gap between her and Gamora's mining pod. Slowly, but surely, her ship edged closer, until Gamora came into firing range. She turned on the ship's communicator, opening all frequencies. She wanted her sister to hear what she was about to say.

"You are a disappointment, sister," Nebula said venomously. "Out of all our siblings, I hated you least."

She hadn't even thought of her other siblings in years. Nebula had been so focused on Gamora for so long, that she had almost forgotten they ever existed.

There was a moment of silence, and then Nebula

heard the sound of Gamora's voice. "Nebula, please," she began. "If Ronan gets the Stone...he'll kill us all!"

"Not all," Nebula replied. "You'll already be dead."

Without another word, Nebula unleashed a single barrage upon Gamora's mining pod. The blast hit the smaller craft, and it burst open in a ball of flame. The ship flew to pieces. There was no way anyone could have survived that explosion, Nebula thought. Not even her charmed sister.

Nebula stared into space, watching Gamora's seemingly lifeless body drifting in the ether.

She was dead, Nebula told herself.

And she felt nothing.

Along with the debris of Gamora's ship, Nebula detected the Orb, floating into space. She locked onto it with a tractor beam, and brought Thanos' prize aboard.

• • •

"The Orb is in my possession, as promised," Ronan

announced to the cracked visage of Thanos displayed on an enormous, some time later. He nodded slightly, beckoning Korath the Pursuer to hold the Orb aloft for their master to see.

"Bring it to me."

Back aboard The Dark Aster, Nebula assumed they would immediately deliver the Orb to her father, fulfilling Ronan's part of the deadly bargain. Thus satisfied, Thanos would then hold up his end of their deadly deal.

She had assumed too much.

"Yes," Ronan continued, "that was our agreement. Bring you the Orb," he said, taking the artifact from Korath's hands, "and you will destroy Xandar for me."

Ronan walked the floor, holding the Orb in his right hand, staring into it longingly. "However, now that I know it contains an Infinity Stone, I wonder what use I have for you."

Nebula suddenly realized they would not be going to see her father after all. For Ronan had just declared war on Thanos.

"Boy," bellowed Thanos, his anger building. "I would reconsider your current course!"

Saying nothing, Ronan twisted the two halves of the Orb, revealing the glowing Infinity Stone inside.

"Master!" Korath shouted, his voice full of panic. "You cannot!"

Nebula thought the same thing. She had heard the stories of the Infinity Stones, and how no living being was capable of harnessing their power. They would consume any person who dared attempt to wield their energies.

Korath's plea fell on deaf ears. Ronan stared at the Infinity Stone, entranced.

"Thanos is the most powerful being in the universe!" Korath protested.

"Not anymore," Ronan stated. With one sweeping motion, he plunged his left hand onto the Infinity Stone, and pulled it away. The Stone appeared embedded in his hand, and Ronan erupted in an unearthly bellow. Energy poured from the Stone, and the floor began to pulsate with an unearthly glow all around him.

Nebula watched. She tilted her head. She wasn't afraid. Not of Ronan. She was curious. Curious as to what would happen to him if he survived this, and about what her father would do to him for this act of ultimate defiance.

Thanos looked on from the screen, as Ronan ordered Korath to give him his weapon. Korath handed it over, and Ronan stared up at Thanos, gloating. Then he slammed the palm of his left hand onto the head of the Cosmi-Rod, embedding the Infinity Stone in its side.

"You call me 'boy?'" thundered Ronan. "I will unfurl a thousand years of Kree justice on Xandar...and burn it to its core!"

Nebula remained silent and still.

"Then, Thanos," Ronan added, "I am coming for you."

There was no reply from the Titan. The screen simply went black.

Ronan turned, and only then did Nebula speak.

"After Xandar," she said, uncertainty in her voice, "you're going to kill my father?"

"You dare oppose me?" Ronan thundered.

Nebula shook her head. He had her all wrong. "You see what he has turned me into," Nebula said. "You kill him, I will help you destroy a thousand planets."

CHAPTER EIGHTEEN

As The Dark Aster entered orbit around Xandar, Nebula looked at the blue world below. So peaceful, so full of life.

Life that would soon come to an end.

Nebula had forgotten what hope felt like, if she ever did know. But now that Ronan possessed the Infinity Stone, he was well his way to fulfilling his own destiny—destroying Xandar. Nebula cared little for that planet or its people. It was the item that came after on Ronan's agenda that now overwhelmed her every thought.

The destruction of Thanos himself.

For the first time in her miserable life, the thought of being freed from Thanos' terrible, polluting influence seemed like a real possibility. The power of the Infinity Stones was unmatched. If Ronan were to confront Thanos, tapping into the Stone's unfathomable power, there was no way the Titan could survive. The Infinity Stone would tear him apart, dispersing his very essence to the four corners of the universe.

What was once a secret dream shared with no one, was now on the verge of becoming reality.

And if she succeeded...

...then what?

With Thanos no more, who was she? Who was Nebula?

She didn't know, and the thought left her cold.

An alert sounded, and Nebula snapped to attention. She checked the scanner and saw the problem—multiple targets rapidly approached The Dark Aster. The ships hadn't launched from Xandar. These had emerged from subspace, right behind Ronan's ship.

Nebula commenced a rapid scan to detect the identity of the new arrivals. A moment later she had her answer, and she walked purposefully toward Ronan's chamber. Inside, the Kree warrior sat on his command chair, shrouded in darkness.

"A fleet approaches," Nebula began. "They appear to be Ravagers."

The Ravagers were known associates of Star-Lord's. Intergalactic scavengers. Thieves. Nebula knew these were not honorable people, nor did they present any type of significant threat against the likes of Ronan. Usually. But if the Ravagers had joined forces with Star-Lord and his team, they might present a real problem. If, somehow, the Ravagers could prevent Ronan from reaching the surface of Xandar, then his plan would be lost.

And Thanos would remain alive.

In order for Ronan's plan to work, the Infinity Stone had to touch the actual, physical surface of Xandar. Once that happened, all life on that world would cease to exist. Plants. Animals. People. All wiped out in the blink of an eye.

Nebula expected some kind of reaction from

Ronan. The man didn't exactly keep his emotions in check, after all. But this time it was different. Perhaps the absolute power of the Infinity Stone had changed him. Whatever the reasoning, Ronan sat calmly in his chair, watching impassively through the enormous window as a wave of Ravager fighters came swooping in for an attack.

The fighters unleashed two fiery plasma bolts right at The Dark Aster. Nebula watched as the blasts hurtled toward their ship. The shots were right on target. There would be no avoiding them. Bracing herself for impact, Nebula looked on with surprise as the plasma bolts collided. The viewing window was eclipsed by an explosion of searing fire. It was all Nebula could see.

She expected the hull to be ruptured, but the fire soon dissipated. Nebula surmised that the plasma bolts had collided with The Dark Aster's invisible shields. The shields held. The plasma bolts were ineffective.

And as the explosion cleared, Nebula could see them. The Ravagers and the Milano, flying beneath The Dark Aster. They'd joined together, just as she'd feared.

She pressed the comms device in her left ear and barked an order: "All pilots—dive! They're beneath us!"

At her command, an entire fleet of small, one-person fighters launched from portals all along The Dark Aster's armored hull. They swooped and darted, rapidly locking onto their Ravager targets.

The aerial battle for the fate of Xandar had begun.

"Forward thrust—now!" Nebula ordered. Ronan's minions engaged The Dark Aster's engines, and the ship roared to life.

What Nebula hadn't known then—what she couldn't have known—was that the rodent who had been accompanying Quill, the ridiculous genetic hybrid, was leading a team of Ravagers who were right then blasting a hole open in The Dark Aster's hull.

What she did know—as it was plainly visible—was that the Xandarian fleet had arrived to aid the opposing side. Their vessels fired upon Ronan's ships. They seemed to be clearing a path toward The Dark Aster.

A path for what? Nebula wondered.

And then she saw it. The Milano. It was coming right for The Dark Aster. Its approach was rapid, then it disappeared from view. Then suddenly, The Dark Aster lurched, as if something collided with it. Later, she would learn that the hole the Ravagers had blasted into The Dark Aster had become a landing bay for the Milano.

All she knew then was that they were being boarded by Peter Quill and his friends.

Another challenge to be faced, Nebula thought to herself. At least her sister, Gamora, would not be among them. She herself had seen Gamora perish in the airless void above Knowhere.

At least she had that victory.

Then why didn't she feel like she had won?

And now, she saw the first signs that her hope to destroy Thanos forever might perish.

"The starboard kern has been breached!" Nebula

roared at Ronan. The urgency in her voice took even Nebula by surprise. "We have been boarded!"

"Continue our approach," Ronan commanded, rising from his seat but with his tone still even. In his right hand, he held the massive hammer that now served as the vessel for the Infinity Stone.

"But the Nova Corps have engaged!"

"None of that will matter once we have reached the surface," Ronan replied coolly.

Nebula did not share Ronan's confidence. She saw he wasn't going to take matters into his own hands—so she would.

"Shield security doors!" she ordered Ronan's minions. "Now!"

A second before the doors slid shut, Nebula screamed at the minions, "Get out of my way!" She raced through the doors, intent on saving her future.

CHAPTER NINETEEN

Eclector M-ship GK9
N42U K11554800·520516
Day 29

I learned something that day.

At least, I think I did.

I would never trust another soul. I swore that, as I stormed off. Not Korath, not Ronan, no one.

Anything I did, anything I would achieve...I would accomplish on my own.

No help from anyone. Others were unreliable at best, incompetent and scheming at worst.

It was ironic, then. After Gamora retrieved me from the Sovereign, and The Milano fell under attack, that I should have to put my trust in her. And her... companions.

I know what she sees in them now, but...

Ugh.

CHAPTER TWENTY

Nebula could not save herself. It was a sobering thought.

Whatever was happening up on the flight deck of The Milano, and outside the ship, it was much worse than before. The explosions outside were more frequent and much closer. Even worse, the ceaseless bickering and arguing from the flight deck continued. It struck her as amazing that even with all the noise inside the ship and out, she could still hear Quill yelling at the rodent, and the rodent yelling back.

The ship was veering back and forth in an ungainly manner, lurching in a stop-start motion. It was so jarring, it felt almost like there were two pilots trying to control the ship at once. Then it dawned on Nebula—that's exactly what must be going on. Quill and the rodent were both trying to pilot the ship because it was in such grave danger, and they both thought they could be the ones to save it. In the process, they would get everyone killed.

"They are morons," she said out loud. There was no one to hear it. There actually had been no one around to hear anything she had to say for a very, very long time.

Nebula realized that, despite the never-ending antagonism they shared, Gamora had always been the one constant presence in Nebula's life. She always listened. Even if she didn't want to...she had no choice. But then she'd run off to join a new family, and it was like Nebula had ceased to matter.

Nebula couldn't feel hurt. But if she could, she would say that it hurt. Just a little.

Nebula jerked backward, as something smashed into the Milano. It wasn't immediately clear what they had struck. Was it a ship? An asteroid? Nebula couldn't tell from her vantage point.

And she didn't have any time to ponder. A second

later, the impact revealed the damage it had caused, as a section of the Milano's stern fell away into space.

Exposed to the vacuum of space, everything that wasn't nailed down in the crew's quarters was sucked backward, and into the void. Clothes, glasses, and food went flying. Nebula was pulled backward as the vacuum did its utmost to get her to join the rest of the crew's quarters in space, her cursed handcuffs the only thing tethering her to the ship—and life.

The cuffs dug into her wrists even more, and Nebula shrieked in pain. It felt like her right arm would be torn from its socket. That would happen long before the cybernetic arm would come apart.

And then there was the oxygen.

Or lack of it.

Thanks to the explosive decompression, all the available oxygen had been evacuated from the crew's quarters. Nebula gasped, but there was nothing to breathe inward.

Suddenly, a yellow energy field appeared, sealing

off the gaping hole in the ship's stern. Atmosphere returned to the crew's quarters, and Nebula fell to the floor in a tangled heap, dangling by her handcuffs. She sucked in a deep lungful of oxygen.

"Idiots!" she screamed.

Nebula could have sworn she heard the rodent say, "Well, that's what you get when Quill flies." But over the roar of the engines, she couldn't be sure.

CHAPTER TWENTY ONE

Eclector M-ship GK9
N42U K11554800·520589
Day 33

I really did call them all idiots.

"The Guardians of the Galaxy."

If the rest of the galaxy could have heard what I heard that day, they wouldn't be so quick to praise them.

Still...

What had Gamora seen in them, four complete strangers, that she didn't—that she couldn't see in me?

I wanted us to be sisters. In every sense of the word.

And if I couldn't have that, well...

CHAPTER TWENTY TWO

"Gamora!" Nebula bellowed as she dropped to the floor. The soles of her shoes made a clang against the metal. "Look at what you have done."

Standing before her were Quill, Drax, and the walking tree.

And Gamora.

Somehow, Gamora had survived. Nebula didn't know how, and she didn't care. All she knew was that the sudden arrival of her sister threatened the one chance she had at living a life on her own terms.

The hallway outside The Dark Aster's flight deck was dark, partly illuminated by strange, glowing lights the tree had produced.

"You have always been weak," Nebula said, ready to strike. "You stupid, traitorous..."

Then the blast hit her. Thrown back by its sheer force, her head landed on the cold metal, and she felt consciousness slipping away. As everything faded to black, she thought she heard Drax say, "Nobody talks to my friends like that."

• • •

Her eyes opened with a start. How long had she been unconscious? Seconds? A minute? She had no idea.

As Nebula stood up, she felt her right arm twist and click back into place. She winced in pain. Parts of that arm were still made of flesh and blood, and hurt as dislocated bones slid back into place. Her cybernetic arm, on the other hand (no pun intended), had crumpled entirely from the impact of the blast. That limb unfurled itself now, and Nebula heard its internal workings rev and whir as the mechanism quickly returned everything to its proper position.

Back on her feet, she looked around, and saw Gamora.

"Nebula, please," Gamora said.

Nebula wasn't having any of what Gamora had to offer. Her sister could never understand what being free of Thanos would mean. She'd always been the favorite, always coddled, at least by Thanos's standards. She wouldn't risk everything to see him destroyed.

But Nebula would.

She took a swipe at her sister with her left arm. Gamora ducked out of the way. Nebula then struck with her right hand. Gamora slipped it, grabbing her, and slamming her in the back.

Gamora ran past, as Nebula went to her knees.

Then Nebula activated the two batons she held in either hand. They extended outward. Looking behind her, she saw Gamora dislodging one of The Dark Aster's power cells. What was Gamora trying to do?

Nebula struck her sister with one of the batons,

and a burst of electricity coursed through Gamora's body. The pain must have been unbearable, Nebula thought.

She hoped it was.

• • •

The two had fought many times before, and nearly always Gamora had won. But today, Nebula had the upper hand. And she pressed it. Stroke after stroke, her batons connected with their mark. Every hit caused a surge of electricity to course through Gamora's nervous system.

Still, Nebula thought, my sister will not fall.

Could she really be so concerned about these people on Xandar that she was willing to risk her life for them? Surely she must realize that she'll die, Nebula thought.

Nebula was so close to winning, so close to finally beating her sister.

If she won, then Ronan would reach his goal.

Xandar would be destroyed, and then it would be Thanos' turn.

But if Nebula lost, then there was the chance Gamora and her friends would stop Ronan, take the Infinity Stone back...and then where would that leave Nebula, but living in a universe where she was nothing. Nothing but an underling in Thanos' elaborate game. Something to be used and discarded.

She swiped at Gamora, who slipped the blow. Even in her battered state, she was still a formidable warrior. Just then, in a burst of strength, Gamora knocked one of the batons from Nebula's hand, taking it for her own.

Weapons crossed and sisters clashed.

She will not win, Nebula swore. Not again. Not ever again.

Another swift stroke from Nebula dislodged Gamora's grip on her weapon. The baton flew out of her hand, and through a gaping hole in the ship's hull behind them. Weaponless, beaten down, Gamora stood her ground.

Nebula showed no mercy. She hit Gamora with everything she had. Gamora stopped the baton right before it hit by slamming her hands together on either side of the weapon. It was now inches away from her face. Nebula pressed the attack, as electricity surged through Gamora's body. She could smell flesh smolder, and Gamora's skeleton was partially visible through her emerald skin as the electric shocks grew stronger.

So close, Nebula thought. Goodbye, sister.

She could see the future before her, a universe without Thanos.

The future vanished as Gamora somehow summoned the will to yank the baton away, and kicked Nebula with all the strength she had left.

Nebula was flung backward, and the ship lurched. She slid down a pile of debris, and toward the gaping hole. Out she went, and as she did, she thrust her left hand upward.

Her left wrist was impaled on a piece of metallic debris, halting her fall. Nebula now dangled from one hand, hanging outside the ship, with nothing but open air and the Xandarian soil below her.

"Nebula!" Gamora shouted. Nebula looked up, and saw her sister coming closer, climbing over the debris. She was trying to reach her. Why? To gloat?

"Sister. Help us fight Ronan," Gamora said, extending her hand. "You know he's crazy!"

Nebula couldn't believe it. After everything... especially now...Gamora still wanted to save her?

Were they not enemies?

Nebula hated Gamora. Gamora hated Nebula. That's just the way it was.

Or...maybe it was...something else?

"I know you're both crazy," Nebula said. Without another word, she disconnected her left hand from her arm, and fell through the sky.

"No!"

She heard Gamora scream from above as she fell, until the sound was drowned out by the air rushing past her ears.

Below her, she saw what she was looking for. But she would have to time it just right.

Her body slammed into the cockpit of the Ravager fighter so hard it caused the ship to veer off-course. Already recovered, Nebula smashed the stump of her left arm through the cockpit, and grabbed the pilot.

"Get out!" she screamed, and, picking up the pilot, threw him through the hole in the cockpit toward the ground below.

The Ravager's ship now hers, Nebula flew away from the battle between Gamora, her friends, the Ravagers, and Ronan.

She knew what would happen. Ronan would lose. It was inevitable. She saw it now.

And then Thanos would be disappointed in his daughter.

Not Gamora.

Never Gamora.

No, he would be disappointed in Nebula. And the

tiniest part of Nebula that still cared just couldn't bear to
be a disappointment one more time.

For the first time in her life, Nebula ran away.

CHAPTER TWENTY THREE

Eclector M-ship GK9
N42U K11554800·520591
Day 33

Everything   I   wanted   was   just   out
of reach.

Everything I thought I wanted?

I   could   have   killed   Gamora   that   day.
I had the chance.

I didn't.

I ran.

I couldn't kill her.

I couldn't face Thanos.

Just...out of my reach.

CHAPTER TWENTY FOUR

It was just out of reach. She was so close. If only she could stretch just a little further...

Suddenly, a black boot kicked the yarrow root away from Nebula, and across the floor.

"It's not ripe," Drax said.

She looked at the tattooed man and suddenly thought she might hate him more than her own sister.

Nebula watched from the floor as Drax reached for a tether coil bolted to the hull. He pulled out the line, and attached it to the back of his belt. Then he grabbed a palm-sized black disc from a shelving unit on the wall. She noticed there was writing beneath it:

SPACESUITS FOR EMERGENCY

Beneath that, someone had scrawled:

Or for fun.

Who are these people? Nebula thought.

Drax reached around and attached the disc to the spot between his shoulder blades. At once, a blue aura projected out from the disc, surrounding Drax's entire body. With this, Nebula knew that Drax would be able to survive in the vacuum of space. Not indefinitely. But long enough for him to accomplish whatever it was he was trying to do.

Which was...what, exactly?

Nebula got to her feet, as she saw Drax remove a rifle from its cradle on the hull.

Was he insane?

Nebula didn't have to wait for her answer.

Drax pressed a large, square button on the wall, and another yellow containment field appeared, separating Nebula and most of the crew's quarters from Drax. He now stood between the two containment barriers. He touched a button on the ceiling and deactivated the field in front of him.

Then he hurled himself into the void.

Nebula stood there stunned, watching, as Drax was dragged behind The Milano, the meager tether his only lifeline.

She saw the fighter trailing The Milano, aiming at the ship. Drax was now trying to fire back.

She knew that The Milano's weapons must not have been functioning, otherwise Quill would have used them to destroy the ship that pursued them. But sending a man outside the ship? With a rifle?

My sister's friends are mad, Nebula thought to herself.

So why did she feel a sense of...admiration, was that it? It crept up on her as she watched Drax's body swing back and forth behind the ship, knocking into asteroids, trying to draw a bead on the enemy.

He fired, and connected. The enemy exploded.

My sister's friends, Nebula thought to herself, are mad, but they're also...impressive.

• • •

It all happened so fast, Nebula hardly knew what to think. One minute, she was watching as Drax destroyed the enemy ship with a rifle. The next, they had jumped through a portal to who knows where. One minute, they were in outer space, the next, it was broad daylight, and The Milano was hurtling toward the ground.

And Drax was still out there, being towed behind the ship.

The Milano had sustained too much damage, and some of its systems began to fail. The containment fields that had prevented Nebula and the rest of the crew's quarters from getting sucked out into space were among the first to go.

Nebula grabbed on to the wall and held on for her life.

Sheets of metal were torn from the hull and sailed past her, out the gaping hole and into the sky, narrowly missing Drax.

Then she saw the tether on the wall. It started to

come loose. In a second, it would tear free, and Drax would be dead.

Nebula dodged another piece of flying metal, and when she looked back up, she saw Gamora racing through the crew's quarters. Just as the tether tore free from the wall, Gamora grabbed it. Then she, too, was nearly sucked out of the ship. At the last second, with one hand grasping the tether, she managed to grab hold of a metal bar at the opening.

Nebula watched as her sister risked being torn in two, trying to save the life of the madman who had shot down a ship in outer space with nothing but a spacesuit and a rifle. Trying to save a maniac.

In that moment, Nebula wondered if she truly had been replaced in Gamora's eyes. If these Guardians were her family now.

Why did even the thought of that hurt so much?

She never tried to save me, Nebula thought. Her. Own. Sister.

CHAPTER TWENTY FIVE

Nebula looked around her in disbelief. Now, The Milano was a real disaster. The ship was in pieces — two, to be precise. What was left of it, anyway. The right wing had been completely severed from the hull and the still attached left wing.

Somehow, miraculously, everyone aboard had survived. Even Drax, who wasn't technically aboard when the ship crashed to surface of the planet Berhert. The ship had plowed through at least a mile of trees before it screeched to a halt, and then promptly fell apart.

Nebula stood in the middle of a clearing in the forest, the smoking wreckage of The Milano behind her. She was surrounded by Quill, Drax, and the rodent. She also noticed a somewhat smaller, almost baby-like version of the tree man she had seen aboard The Dark Aster. Was it the same creature?

Then there was Gamora. She walked around the wreckage, fuming.

"Look at this! Where's the other half of our ship?" Gamora demanded.

Peter Quill tried to remain calm. "My ship," he interjected.

Gamora wasn't having it. "Either one of you could have gotten us through that field."

So I was right, Nebula thought. It was some ridiculous competition between Quill and the rodent that ultimately led to our crash.

"Peter...we almost died because of your arrogance," Gamora said.

Quill pointed an angry finger at the rodent. "More like because he stole Anulax batteries!"

Wait, Nebula thought—the rodent had stolen Anulax batteries, too? Those batteries were the whole reason she had fallen into Gamora's custody. Nebula had attempted to steal the batteries from the Sovereign. Their civilization depended upon the Anulax batteries for their power. Consequently, they were worth a great deal of units.

"You know why I did it, Star-Munch? Mmm?" the rodent said, goading Quill.

"I'm not gonna answer to 'Star-Munch,'" Quill said, attempting to walk away.

Then Nebula watched as the rodent got right in Quill's face, shouting, "I did it because I wanted to! What are we even talking about this for? We just had a little man save us by blowing up 50 ships!"

A little man? Nebula thought. What is this demented furball talking about?

As if in answer, Drax asked, "How little?"

The rodent pinched the thumb and forefinger on his left hand together.

Gamora rolled her eyes. "A little one-inch man saved us?"

The rodent shrugged. "Well, if he got closer, I'm sure he'd be much larger."

The conversation kept on in this fashion for more minutes than Nebula cared to count. Nebula, who had seen so much, experienced so much, had never seen anything like it. The excessive bantering didn't seem to serve any point. Everyone was getting on one another's nerves, and she couldn't understand why someone didn't just attack and end it.

Finally, Quill said something that was clearly meant as an insult toward the rodent, and the furry thing leapt at Star-Lord.

Now that, Nebula thought, I understand.

Just as the two were about to get into it, Nebula raised her head skyward. She heard it first—rather, her cybernetic hearing detected it before anyone else in the group. A ship descending through the upper atmosphere, rapidly approaching their exact location.

"Someone followed you through the jump point!" Nebula warned as she pointed toward the sky. The rodent took the safety off his weapon, and Drax hoisted the rifle he had been carrying. Everyone stood with their backs toward one another, forming a tight circle as they looked skyward.

"Set me free," Nebula said softly to Gamora, lifting her hands to indicate her still-cuffed wrists. "You'll need my help!"

"I'm not a fool, Nebula."

"You are a fool if you deprive yourself of a hand in combat," Nebula replied.

Above, a ship quickly became visible—white, oval, descending overhead.

"You'd attack me the moment I let you go," Gamora said, shrugging off Nebula's request.

"No I won't." Even Nebula had to admit it didn't sound remotely convincing.

"You know, you'd think an evil super-villain would learn how to properly lie," Quill answered.

Nebula paused. She didn't know how to lie. She

never learned. The price for lying to her father was death. Needless to say, it was a skill she had never acquired.

Nebula and the Guardians of the Galaxy watched apprehensively as a ship the shape and color of an egg crushed the trees on its descent and finally came to a stop. A moment later, a doorway opened, and out walked a humanoid woman with two antenna atop her forehead, and a bearded man, seemingly human.

"After all these years, I've found you," said the bearded man, looking at Quill.

Who is he? Nebula wondered.

"Who the hell are you?" Quill asked.

"I figured my rugged good looks would make that obvious. My name is Ego," the bearded man said with a benevolent smile. "I'm your dad, Peter."

Fathers, thought Nebula with a roll of her eyes.

CHAPTER TWENTY SIX

"You're just going?" Nebula said in disbelief.

"I'm not 'just' going," Gamora said, as she filled a backpack with rations. "If this really is Peter's father, then he needs to know more about him. Spend time with him." Several hours had passed since Ego had first introduced himself to the group and invited Peter back to his planet. Peter had agreed to go, with Drax and Gamora accompanying him, while the rest of the group stayed behind to fix The Milano.

Nebula grunted. "I'm sure he'll be wonderful, just like our father."

"No one's like Thanos," Gamora shot back. She looked up at her sister from where she was crouched, packing up her belongings. "Why didn't you let me save you back aboard The Dark Aster? All you had to do was take my hand."

Nebula stood in the crew's quarters, and looked over at Rocket. She learned that the rodent had a name, loathe as she was to actually use it. He was minding his own business, hard at work reconstructing The Milano, piece by piece. It would take days, but eventually, the ship would be restored, and hopefully, space-worthy once again.

"You ask me that," Nebula said, not looking at her sister. "And if I answer, you would not possibly understand."

"How do you know that I won't?" Gamora replied. "Wasn't I raised by Thanos, just like you?"

"No one was raised just like me," Nebula said, her voice trailing off.

• • •

"You're leaving me with that fox?!?" Nebula roared.

Gamora picked up her bag and walked away from Nebula. "Shoot her if she does anything suspicious," she said to Rocket.

Rocket barely acknowledged Gamora; he just kept on working.

Nebula stood there for a long time after Gamora and the others had left, wondering what she would do for the next few days waiting for her sister to return. The thought of being stuck in the ship with the furball and the tree was repellent.

What has happened to me? she thought. I was poised to destroy worlds, overthrow my father for control of the universe. Then? Incarcerated by the Sovereign for petty thievery. Captured by my sister, forced to live among her insipid companions.

Why have I not killed her yet?

And why am I...why am I questioning everything?

Nebula was so used to finding strength and resolve in her anger and hatred, that she wasn't sure how to move forward. For the first time in her life, she seemed to have no purpose. She wasn't being forced to compete against her sister for the favor of their father. Nor was she beholden to someone like Ronan. She was responsible to no one, save herself.

The thought frightened her.

Nebula slowly sat down in a chair. Uneasy, she looked at the wall, and saw a blaster resting in a cradle. She could reach it in no time, she thought. It would be an easy matter to grab the weapon, aim it at the rodent, then—

"If you're thinkin' about grabbin' that rifle off the wall and shootin' me with it, think again," Rocket said, not looking up from his repair work. "I'll be on you before you can so much as think about squeezing the trigger. And I bite."

Nebula leaned back in her chair, and sighed. "I'm sure you do," she said.

CHAPTER TWENTY SEVEN

Eclector M-ship GK9
N42U K11554800·520634
Day 38

Why didn't I take Gamora's hand? She was right. It would have been easy. Just reach up. Grab it. Join her. Become the sisters...the family we never had been.

I wanted that. Very much.

I wanted a sister. The one who, many years ago, had tried to help me.

I couldn't bring myself to do it.

Hanging from The Dark Aster, my only hope of ever being free of Thanos began to dwindle away into nothingness. The only chance of destroying Thanos and ending his power over me once and for all lay in Ronan and the Infinity Stone. As the tide of battle had turned, it was clear that Ronan might lose, and the Infinity Stone might be taken from him.

Only with the Infinity Stone could Ronan stop Thanos. Without it...

How could I have taken her hand, and agree to help Gamora stop Ronan, when it would mean destroying my only chance at a life worth living?

How could I ever look her in the eye, knowing that every time , I would see the person who had doomed me to a dismal existence, however unintentionally and without malice?

There was already so much history between us. So much that was unspoken. So much anger.

I couldn't add that to the list.

So I let go.

After I commandeered the Ravager's craft, I got as far away from Xandar as I could. I wanted to run, to crawl off somewhere...

...to hide.

But from whom? Thanos? Gamora?

Or myself?

CHAPTER TWENTY EIGHT

"You make a better wall than a window."

"What?"

Nebula whirled around, her thoughts suddenly interrupted. Standing right in front of her was the rodent.

"It means I can't see through you," Rocket said, annoyed. "Can you move? I can't fix things I can't see."

Nebula grunted, then moved away from the control panel in front of which she had been standing. She had lost track of time, pondering her thoughts. She wasn't used to the luxury of thinking, of even having private thoughts. All her life, she had lived in the Sanctuary with Thanos. Only until recently had she been assigned to Ronan's charge. There was no such thing as privacy, or thoughts that belonged only to her.

"Just to let you know," Rocket said, as he went to work on the panel, "I don't like talkin'."

"You talk all the time," Nebula said.

"Yeah, but I don't like it," Rocket replied.

"Then why do it?" Nebula asked.

"Because if I don't talk, everyone will just think I'm a dumb animal," he said.

Nebula thought for a moment. "You're not a dumb animal," she said.

Rocket stopped what he was doing, and stared at Nebula. "Did you just say something nice to me?"

"No," Nebula said, turning away from Rocket.

"Quill's right," Rocket said, starting up his repairs once more, now with a rare, small smile playing about his furry features. "For a bad guy, you're a lousy liar."

CHAPTER TWENTY NINE

The sound of gunfire startled Nebula, jarring her from the first sound, dreamless sleep she'd had in who knows how long. She sat up, her hands still cuffed. She saw the little tree creature staring out a window, looking at what was happening outside.

She looked for Rocket.

He wasn't there.

Instantly, she realized what happened. Someone else had arrived, and was trying to destroy the Guardians. Or capture them.

Rocket must have gone out to meet them.

Suddenly, she heard the sound of more

gunfire. It sounded as though it was a little ways away from the ship, and it echoed through the trees.

Then there was the sound of concussion mines. Screams followed.

• • •

The sounds of fighting grew closer to The Milano. But handcuffed as she was, Nebula wasn't able to pull herself over to the window to see what was happening. Then she heard a voice she recognized.

Rocket.

"How's it going, you blue idiot," he said.

"Not so bad," came a voice she didn't know. "We got ourselves a pretty good little gig here. This golden gal with quite a high opinion of herself has offered us a large sum to deliver you and your pals over to her because she wants to kill y'all."

The sound of people laughing followed.

A lot of people.

"Your friend," Nebula said to the tree creature. "There's too many of them. He needs my help. If you care about him, you need to get me out of these bonds." She held up her hands, and showed the handcuffs to Groot. The tree creature didn't seem to know what it should do.

"They are going to kill him!" Nebula pleaded.

She almost convinced herself that she was being honest with Groot.

• • •

She saw the blue man with the red stripe on his head, standing in the middle of a circle of men. Rocket was there, too. Everyone had their weapons leveled at the rodent. Nebula figured the man with the red stripe was the leader, the men his crew.

Except the crew seemed to be in a state of mutiny. There was heated debate over the one with the red stripe who she heard them call Yondu having "gone soft" by letting Quill get away with whatever he wanted or some such. These must be the Ravagers, she thought. She could feel the tide turning, and realized that Yondu might be the key to her way off this planet, to get what she wanted.

A full-scale fight threatened to break out, and Nebula couldn't have that.

Hidden from everyone, she fired the first shot. It hit Yondu right in the stripe on his head, and there was a burst of electricity. He hit the ground, unconscious.

Then she fired again, incapacitating Rocket.

At last, she revealed herself, as the Ravagers turned her way.

"Well, hello boys," she said. Blaster in her right hand, she held a yarrow root in her left hand—hook, really. For all she knew, her cybernetic left hand was still attached to the remains of The Dark Aster.

She raised the yarrow root to her mouth, and took a big bite. A second later, she spat it out.

"It's not ripe," she said.

CHAPTER THIRTY

Eclector M-ship GK9
N42U K11554800·520705
Day 44

I regret shooting the fox.

No. Not "the fox." He has a name.

Rocket.

Why did I do that? There must have been another way. Gamora would have found another way.

But that's the only way I've ever known.

We act according to who we are.

That's who I was then.

Am I different now?

I would like to think so.

CHAPTER THIRTY ONE

By wounding Yondu, Nebula had given the mutineers exactly what they wanted—control over their own destiny. And over their ship, the Eclector.

She had also given them Rocket and the young Groot. They would be handed over to the Sovereign, and the Ravagers would reap the reward. Rocket and Groot would pay the ultimate price for daring to steal the Anulax batteries. The irony of two "Guardians of the Galaxy" forced to endure the same punishment that should have been hers did not escape Nebula.

In return, the Ravagers gave her the fastest ship they had, along with the coordinates of Ego's homeworld programmed into its navigation system.

She was done running away.

As she sat behind the controls of the ship, Nebula knew what she had to do.

Once and for all, Gamora must die.

• • •

Most people, when they're angry at their sibling, don't fly a spaceship into a cave with weapons blazing, not caring if they crash, not caring if they live or die, as long as they destroy the sibling with whom they're currently furious.

Nebula wasn't most people.

Arriving in the upper atmosphere of Ego's homeworld, Nebula locked in on her sister. It was an easy matter to locate her distinct energy signal. Once she had, she went in with weapons lit and an attitude to match.

There she was, standing in the middle of a field. So alone. So helpless.

Nebula knew the feeling.

Her craft swooping on, she opened upon her

sister, chasing her into a deep cave, tearing the Ravager ship to bits on the cavern walls as she flew it apart.

She didn't care.

Nebula screamed as the ship crashed along the cavern floor, coming to a halt right at huge crevasse. Stunned, equipment sparking around her, she gasped for air.

From the shattered cockpit, Nebula groaned. She was pinned beneath the wreckage. Looking out from the cockpit, she saw Gamora. Still alive.

Always alive.

Then she watched, helpless, as her sister hefted an enormous weapon—one of the Ravager ship's guns that had broken during the crash. She lifted the gun to her shoulder, and opened fire on Nebula.

Then Gamora threw down the gun.

She made her way over to the cockpit, and reached inside. She pulled Nebula free from the wreckage, just as the ship exploded. The sheer force of the blast threw the two women backward, and they landed on the hard, rocky surface of the cavern.

Both women groaned, exhausted.

Which was the perfect moment for Nebula to attack.

"Are you kidding me?!?" Gamora shouted, as Nebula pressed her advantage by rolling over onto Gamora and beginning to rain blows down upon her.

After a quick exchange of blows, Nebula caught Gamora's neck with her left hand. She squeezed as hard as she could, and felt her sister's windpipe begin to give way.

Gamora gasped, unable to breathe. Nebula pulled a dagger from the holster on her hip and held it in her right hand. She raised it, ready to strike. To drive it through Gamora, and end her. End everything.

For Nebula, time came to a standstill. She felt like she had stepped outside herself, and was watching.

A spectator, as one sister tried to kill another.

If she squeezed her throat just a little harder...if

she could only bring herself to plunge the dagger through her eye...then it would all be over. The hate, the anger...it would be gone. She was sure of it.

What was she waiting for? Thanos to come and watch? To say, "You've done well, Nebula. You are my favorite daughter?"

That would never happen. No matter how hard she tried, Nebula would never be recognized by her father. He would never be her true family.

There was only one person in her life who could fill that role. And she was currently pinned beneath her, gasping for air.

Nebula dropped the dagger and released her grip on Gamora.

"I win," Nebula announced, her breath coming in short bursts from the effort of pinning down her sister. "I win. I bested you in combat."

"No," Gamora said, holding her throat. "I saved your life."

"Well you were stupid enough to let me live,"

Nebula replied. She sat there on the rocky surface of the cavern, panting, catching her breath.

Gamora glared at her sister. "You let me live!"

"I don't need you always trying to beat me!" Nebula roared.

"I'm not the one who flew across the universe just because I wanted to win," Gamora shot back.

"Do not tell me what I want!"

"I don't need to tell you what you want," Gamora raged. "It's obvious!"

Nebula knew then that Gamora had no idea.

"You were the one who wanted to win," Nebula said. She sounded tired. "I just wanted a sister."

Suddenly, Gamora had nothing to say.

"You were all I had," Nebula said, feeling the words bursting out of her. "You were the one who needed to win. Thanos pulled my eye from my head..."

Nebula could barely get the words out now.

"...and my brain from my skull...and my arm from my body."

Gamora looked at Nebula, not knowing what to say.

"Because. Of. You," Nebula finished. The two women stood facing each other, not speaking.

There was nothing left to say.

CHAPTER THIRTY TWO

Nebula was leaving. It was over. She had traveled to Ego's world to have it out with Gamora once and for all, and ended up...

...what? Confessing. Revealing her innermost thoughts. Her fears. She showed weakness before her sister.

And yet, she lived. Nothing terrible had happened. Gamora had not used that weakness against her, had not tried to turn it into some kind of victory that would have resulted in yet another part being plucked from Nebula's body and replaced with a cybernetic facsimile.

Along with the Guardians, she had returned to the Ravager ship, Eclector. They had defeated Peter's father, Ego. The world was destroyed. Now, she was heading off to face an uncertain future, taking a Ravager M-ship to do the impossible.

As she walked toward the docking bay, Nebula heard her sister call her name.

"Nebula."

Taking a deep breath, she turned around. Gamora stood there, silent.

Nebula waited. If her sister had anything to say to her, now was the time.

"I was a child like you," Gamora said, tentatively, softly. "I was concerned with staying alive until the next day, every day. And I never considered what Thanos was doing to you."

She couldn't believe the words she was hearing. Nebula never knew she wanted—needed—to hear them.

"I'm trying to make it right," Gamora said, staring into Nebula's eyes. "There are little girls like you across the universe who are in danger. You can stay with us and help them."

A home.

A part of Nebula wanted this to be a brand-new beginning for her and her sister. Together.

But she knew it wasn't to be.

That was Gamora's story. Nebula needed to find her own.

"I will help them," Nebula said. "By killing Thanos."

A look of sadness crossed Gamora's face. "I don't know if that's possible."

Nebula said nothing. She simply turned away. Then she felt a hand on her shoulder, whirling around in self-defense, she was stunned to find that Gamora wasn't trying to restrain her or to attack her.

She was...hugging her.

It was the first time Gamora had hugged her sister since...ever.

Nebula hardly knew how to react. For the longest time, she just stood there, arms at her sides.

At long last, Gamora pulled back and said, her eyes glazed with tears: "You will always be my sister."

EPILOGUE

Something happened that day that I thought would never occur.

And in turn I did something which I thought myself incapable of doing.

My sister hugged me.

I hugged her.

And I did not attempt to shove a dagger into her back.

I am still angry.

I am still full of hate.

But I direct those feelings now at my father, and my father alone.

The time is very nearly at hand. I am closer than I have ever been. There will be a reckoning between us. Thanos will be made to feel the pain of each and every organ that he plucked from my body, and he will know despair.

And then at long last, I will finally be free to live my life.

Free.